Dear Parent:
Your child's love of reading starts here!

Every child learns to read in a different way and at his or her own speed. Some go back and forth between reading levels and read favorite books again and again. Others read through each level in order. You can help your young reader improve and become more confident by encouraging his or her own interests and abilities. From books your child reads with you to the first books he or she reads alone, there are I Can Read Books for every stage of reading:

SHARED READING
Basic language, word repetition, and whimsical illustrations, ideal for sharing with your emergent reader

BEGINNING READING
Short sentences, familiar words, and simple concepts for children eager to read on their own

READING WITH HELP
Engaging stories, longer sentences, and language play for developing readers

READING ALONE
Complex plots, challenging vocabulary, and high-interest topics for the independent reader

ADVANCED READING
Short paragraphs, chapters, and exciting themes for the perfect bridge to chapter books

I Can Read Books have introduced children to the joy of reading since 1957. Featuring award-winning authors and illustrators and a fabulous cast of beloved characters, I Can Read Books set the standard for beginning readers.

A lifetime of discovery begins with the magical words **"I Can Read!"**

Visit www.icanread.com for information
on enriching your child's reading experience.

To Shira and Zohar

HarperCollins®, 🖼®, and I Can Read Book® are trademarks of HarperCollins Publishers Inc.

Library of Congress Cataloging-in-Publication Data

Karlin, Nurit.

The fat cat sat on the mat / written and illustrated by Nurit Karlin.

p. cm.—(An I can read book)

Summary: Rat tries to get the fat cat off the mat and back to his usual resting place in the vat.

ISBN-10: 0-06-026673-2 (trade bdg.) — ISBN-13: 978-0-06-026673-8 (trade bdg.)

ISBN-10: 0-06-026674-0 (lib. bdg.) — ISBN-13: 978-0-06-026674-5 (lib. bdg.)

ISBN-10: 0-06-444246-2 (pbk.) — ISBN-13: 978-0-06-444246-6 (pbk.)

[1. Cats—Fiction. 2. Rats—Fiction. 3. Witches—Fiction. 4. Brooms and brushes—Fiction. 5. Stories in rhyme.] I. Title. II. Series.

PZ3.K1266Fat 1996   95-25952

[E]—dc20   CIP

18 19 20 LSCC 60 59 58 57 56 55 54   AC

❖

I Can Read!

BEGINNING
1
READING

THE FAT CAT SAT ON THE MAT

WITHDRAWN

written and illustrated by
NURIT KARLIN

HarperCollins*Publishers*

Wilma the witch has a crazy broom.

It likes to fly around her room.

She also has a fat cat

and a pet rat.

Wilma loves her pet rat.

She calls the rat

"my little brat."

The rat hates the cat.

The cat does not care.

The cat, who is fat,

just lies in the vat

and stares at the rat.

The rat hates that.

One night, when Wilma was out,
the fat cat got out of the vat.
He went, *pit-a-pat*,
and sat on the mat.

"This is MY mat!" said the rat.

"So what," said the cat.

"So get off!" said the rat.

"No I won't," said the cat.

"Then I will go and get my bat,"
said the rat.

"It will get you off the mat."

"No it won't," said the cat.

"This is the mat of the rat,"
said the bat.

"So what," said the cat.

"So get off!" said the bat.

"No I won't," said the cat.

"Then I will go and get my hat,"
said the bat.

"It will get you off the mat."

"No it won't," said the cat.

"This is the mat of the rat,"
said the hat.

"So what," said the cat.

"So get off!" said the hat.

"No I won't," said the cat.

"I am a cat, and I am fat.
No rat, no bat, no hat
can move me.
I shall sit on this mat
for as long as I wish."

"We shall see," said the hat.

15

"Look what we have," said the hat.

"Big deal, a dish," said the cat.

"A dish and what else?" asked the hat.

"Mmmm . . . a fish!" said the cat.

"A fish on a dish," said the hat.

"For me?" asked the cat.

"Yes, for you," said the hat.

"Bring it closer," said the cat.

"Come and get it," said the hat.

"You think I am stupid,"
said the cat.

"You want to get me off the mat.

I won't get off, and that is that!"

Rat-a-tat . . .

"What was that?" asked the bat.

"I don't know," said the hat.

Rat-a-tat . . .

"It sounds like a rat with a tat,"
said the cat.

"It is not me," said the rat.

"What is a tat?" asked the bat.

"I don't know," said the hat.

"Look! The broom!" cried the bat.

The broom flew into the room.

It zoomed over the mat,

over the cat,

over the hat and the bat

and Wilma's pet rat.

The fish flew off the dish.

It landed on the hat,

which landed on the bat,

who landed on the rat,

who landed on the cat,

lying flat on the mat.

"Get off!" said the cat.

"No we won't!" said the hat
and the bat and the rat.

The fish said nothing.

Wilma came home.

She looked at the room.

She picked up the broom.

Then she asked,

"Why is the fish out of the dish?"

"Because of the cat," said the rat.

"The fat cat sat on my mat!"

"My dear little brat," said Wilma,

"what makes you think

this is YOUR mat?"

The fat cat smiled.

The fat cat got up

and stretched.

Off flew the rat, the bat,

and the hat.

He ate the fish,

    licked the dish,

        and went back

            to lie down in the vat.

"Thank goodness!"

said the mat.